WITHDRAWN

Alfred A. Knopf
New York

WALLY DOES NOT WANT A HAIRCUT

AMANDA DRISCOLL

Wally did not need a haircut.
His hair was perfectly fine.

Sure, it tripped him up a tad, gathered a bit of greenery, and made hoedowns a little hazardous.

And Wally DID miss hugging his mama.

Still . . . Wally did NOT need a haircut.
Nobody could make him get one.

"High time for a haircut, Wally," said Mama.
The scissors went

SWICKA! SWICKA!

Wally winced.

The shears went

BZZT! BZZT!

Wally wiggled.

"Now hold real still."

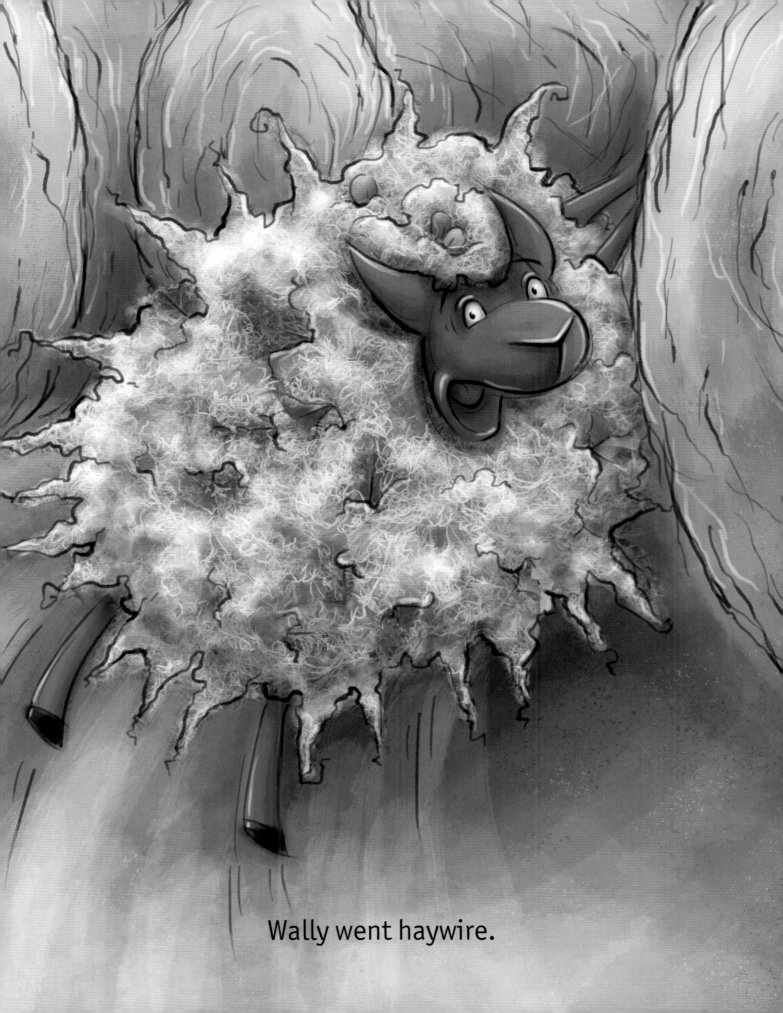

Wally went haywire.

"I see you hiding, Wally," said Mama. "Don't worry, little lamb, haircuts don't hurt. Watch me," she said. Soon Mama's hair looked ooh-la-la.

"Check this out, Wally,"
said Sheepdog.
Soon Sheepdog sported
a stylish new 'do.

Before long, all the animals joined in.
Shears ZIPPITY-ZIP-ZIPPED.
Scissors SNIPPETY-SNIP-SNIPPED.

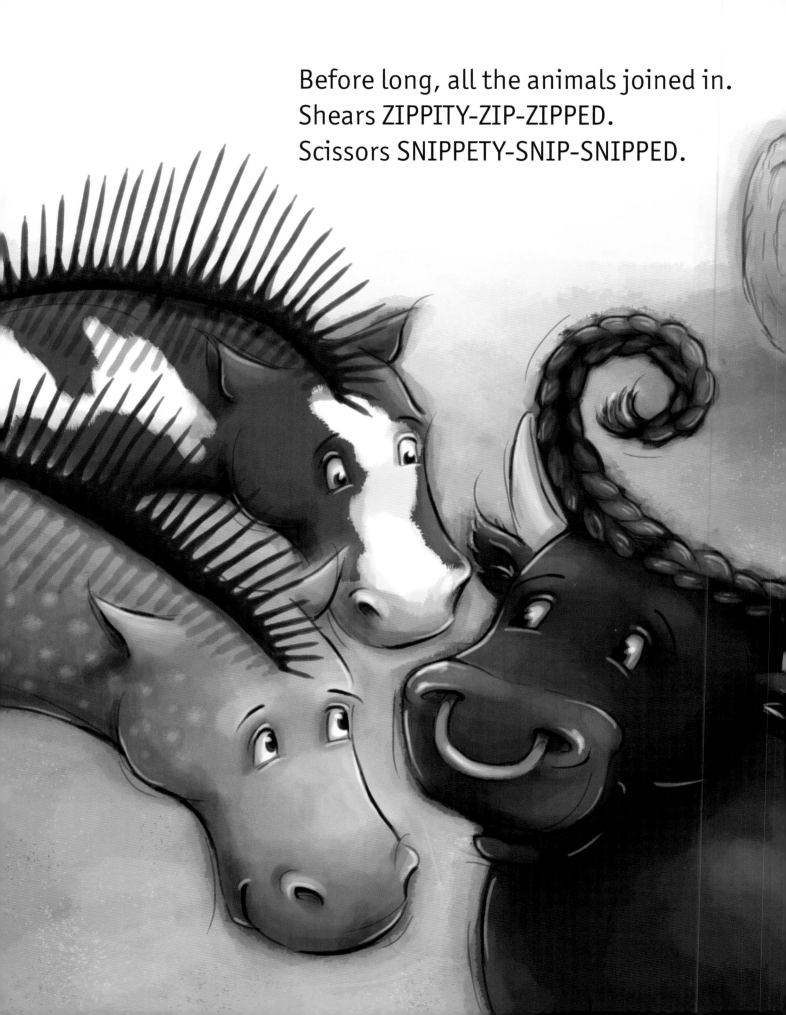

Goats got top knots,
bulls wore braids,
and horses rocked Mohawks.
Wally watched warily.

Cows got curls,

donkeys
donned updos,

and the yak
sported spikes.

Even the pigs wore wigs.

"Let's party!"
hollered the animals.
Everyone danced
the haircut hoedown.

Everyone except Wally.

Mama appeared at Wally's side. "I'd love to dance with my favorite partner," she said.

Wally grinned and tried to move,
but his hair was tangled in the hay.

 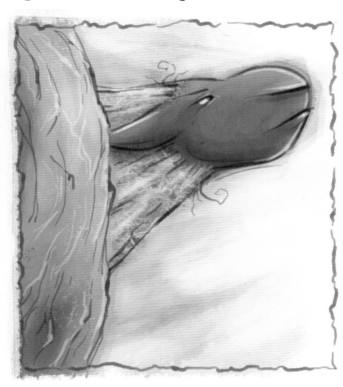

He squirmed. He shimmied. He stretched.

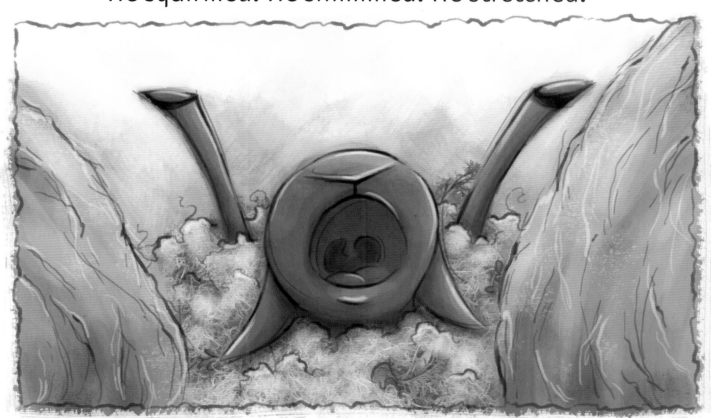

"I'm stuck!"

"Don't panic," said Mama.
"We'll get you out."
All the animals helped.

They used horse power,
a battering ram, and
dogged determination.
But Wally's hair held.

Then Wally spied the scissors. He had no other choice. "Uh . . . Mama . . . will you cut my hair?" Wally said sheepishly. "With pleasure," said Mama.

Wally took a deep breath. Mama snipped. It didn't hurt. She snipped some more. "Not ba-a-a-d," said Wally.

"I'm free!" said Wally,
dancing the trimmed-up two-step.

Wally twirled without tripping . . .
glided without gathering greenery . . .

and became the hero of the hoedown.

Then he did the one thing he had missed most.

Wally hugged his mama.

For Maddie and Jack,
with heartfelt hugs and limitless love

THIS IS A BORZOI BOOK PUBLISHED BY ALFRED A. KNOPF

Copyright © 2016 by Amanda Driscoll

All rights reserved. Published in the United States by Alfred A. Knopf,
an imprint of Random House Children's Books, a division of Penguin Random House LLC, New York.
Knopf, Borzoi Books, and the colophon are registered trademarks of Penguin Random House LLC.

Visit us on the Web! randomhousekids.com

Educators and librarians, for a variety of teaching tools, visit us at RHTeachersLibrarians.com

Library of Congress Cataloging-in-Publication Data
Driscoll, Amanda, author, illustrator.
Wally does not want a haircut / Amanda Driscoll.—First edition.
p.   cm
Summary: Wally the sheep does not want to get the haircut he really needs, even after all the other farm animals
get new hairdos, but when his shaggy wool gets him in trouble, he has no choice but to ask for a trim.
ISBN 978-0-553-53579-2 (trade) — ISBN 978-0-553-53580-8 (lib. bdg.) — ISBN 978-0-553-53581-5 (ebook)
[1. Haircutting—Fiction. 2. Sheep—Fiction. 3. Domestic animals—Fiction.] I. Title.
PZ7.D7866Wal 2016
[E]—dc23
2014040511

The illustrations in this book were created using pencil sketches painted in Adobe Photoshop.

MANUFACTURED IN MALAYSIA
July 2016   10 9 8 7 6 5 4 3 2 1   First Edition